hic,
hic,
hic

To Kiko
—M. C.

To Susan—my online savvy shopper who found
me the best bones
—S. D. S.

Margaret K. McElderry Books
An imprint of Simon & Schuster Children's Publishing Division
1230 Avenue of the Americas
New York, NY 10020
Text copyright © 2002 by Margery Cuyler
Illustrations copyright © 2002 by S. D. Schindler
Book design by Kristin Smith
The text of this book is set in Caxton.
The illustrations are rendered in gouache, watercolor, and ink.
Manufactured in China   1120 SCP
20 19 18 17

Library of Congress Cataloging-in-Publication Data
Cuyler, Margery
Skeleton hiccups / Margery Cuyler ; illustrated by S. D. Schindler.— 1st ed.
p. cm.
Summary: Ghost tries to help Skeleton get rid of the hiccups.
ISBN 978-0-689-84770-7
[1. Hiccups—Fiction. 2. Ghosts—Fiction. 3. Skeleton—Fiction.] I. Schindler,
S. D. ill. II. Title.
PZ7.C997 Sk 2002
[E]—dc21
2001044121

SKeLeToN hiCcups

by margery cuyler

illustrated by S. d. schindler

Margaret K. McElderry Books

New York London Toronto Sydney Singapore

Skeleton woke up.

hic,
hic,
hic

Had the hiccups.   hic, hic, hic

Took a shower.

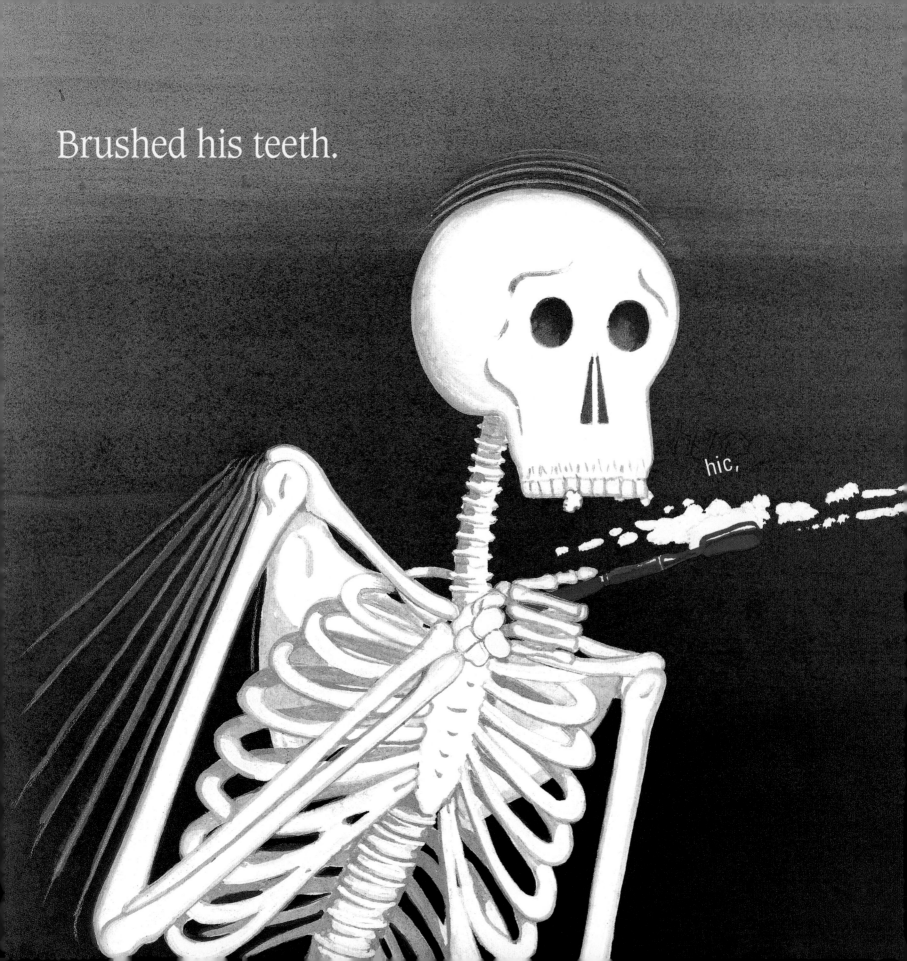

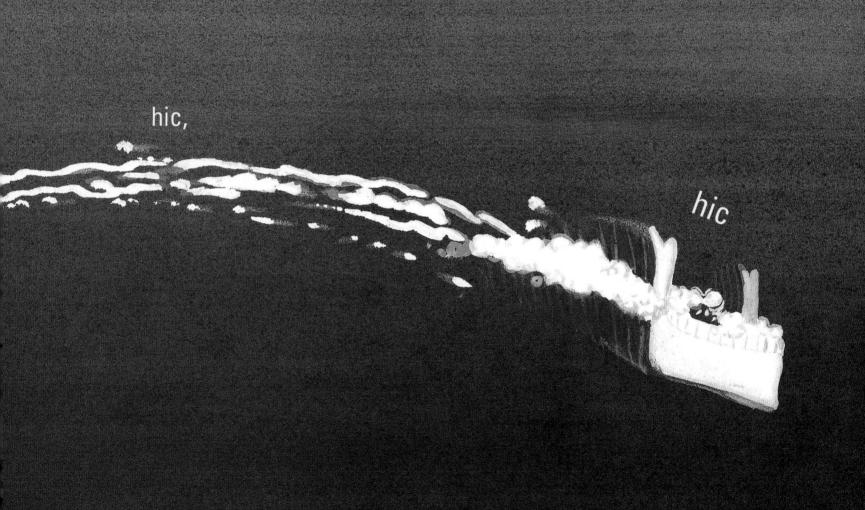

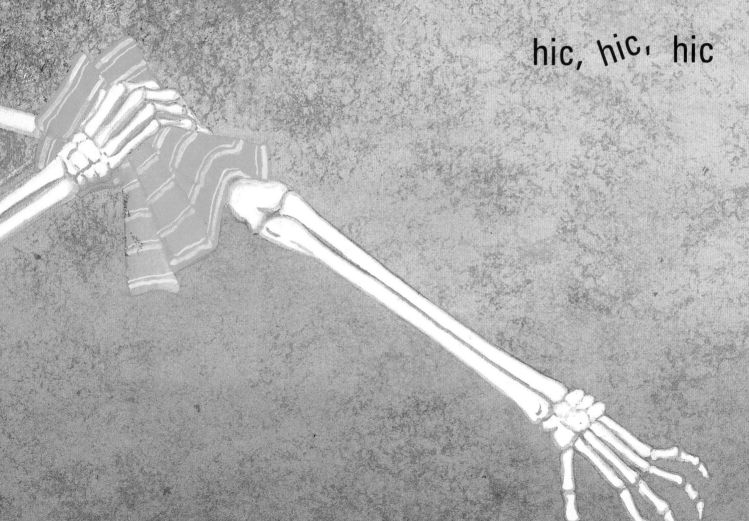

Polished his bones.

hic, hic, hic

Carved a pumpkin.

Raked some leaves.

hic,

hic,

hic

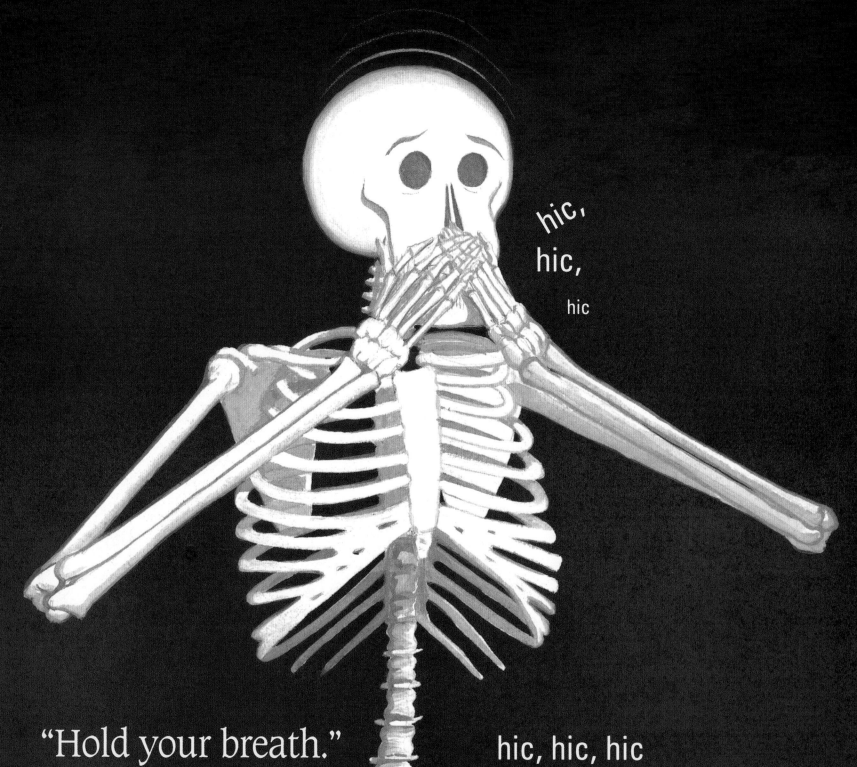

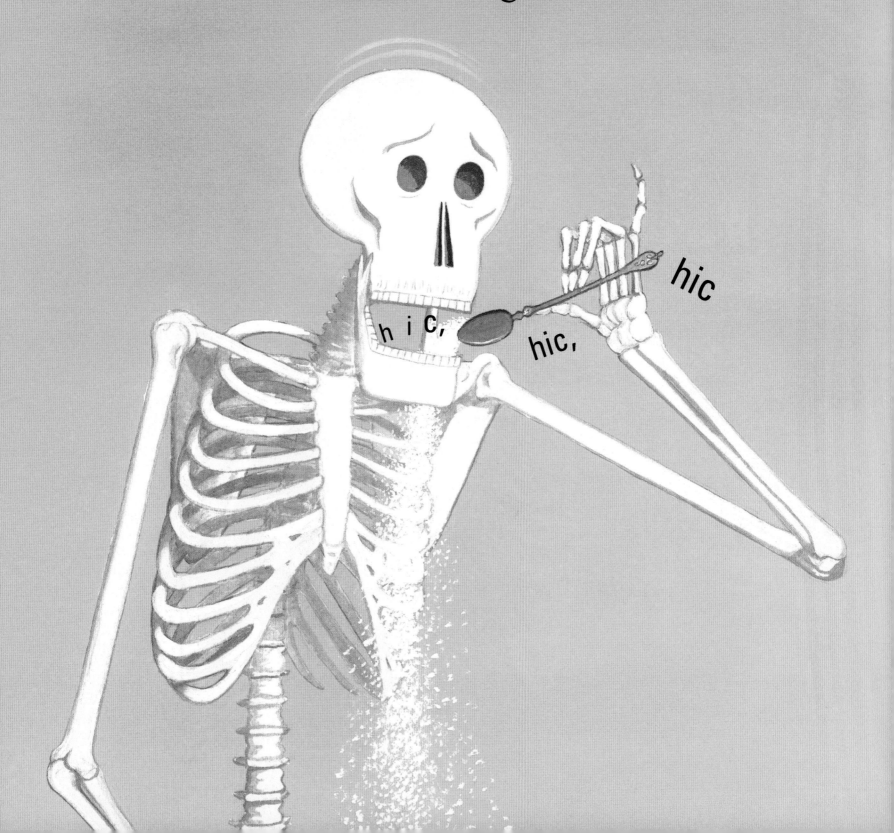

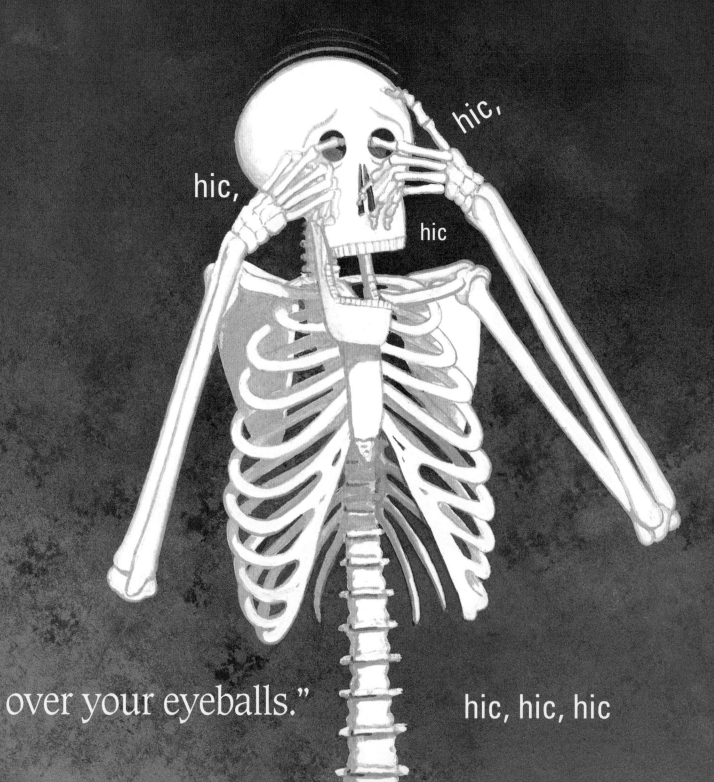

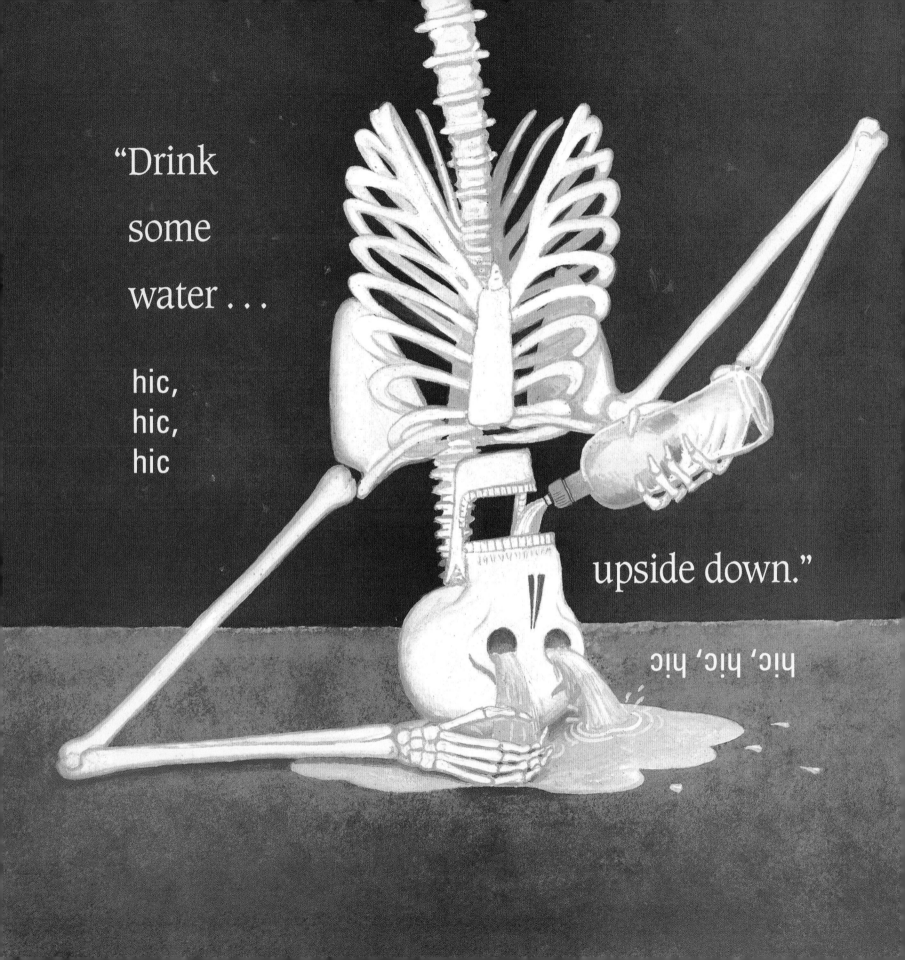

Ghost made a face.

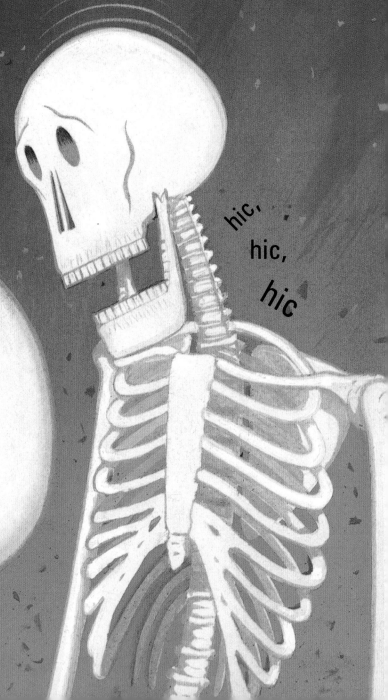

hic,
hic,

hic

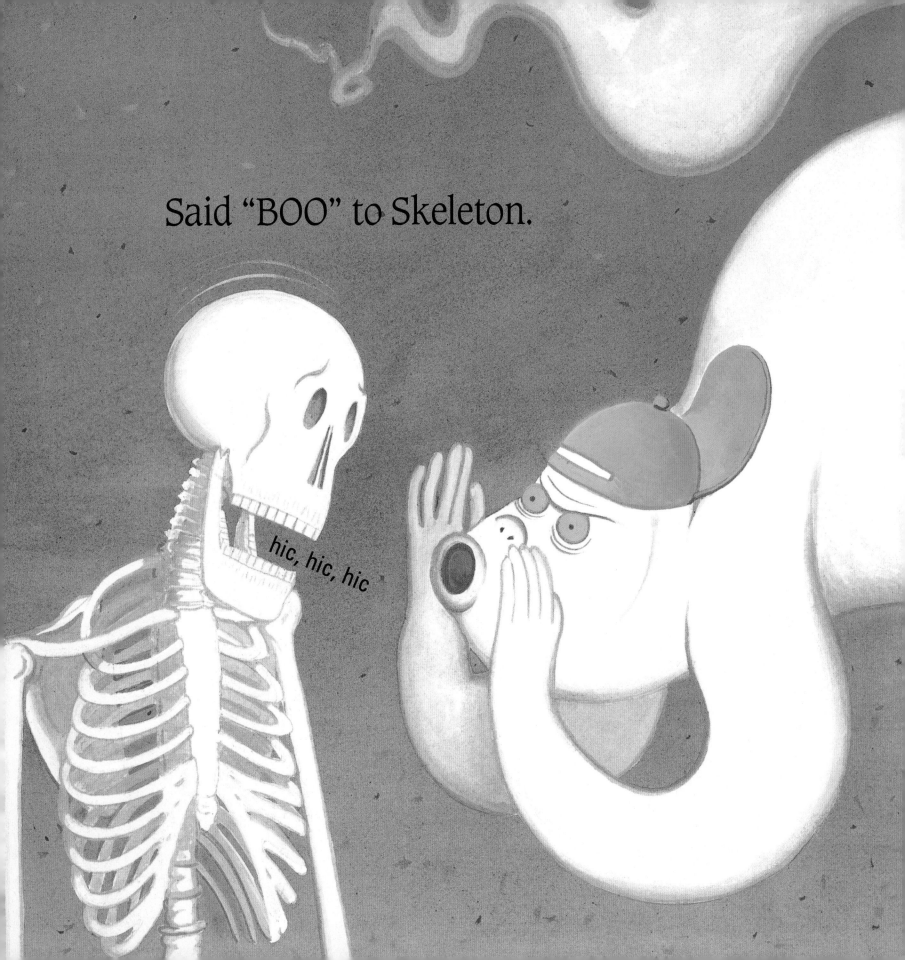

Said "BOO" to Skeleton.

hic, hic, hic

But nothing worked.

hic, hic, **hic**

The hiccups
stayed.

hic,

hic,

hic

Then Ghost got smart.

hic, hic, hic

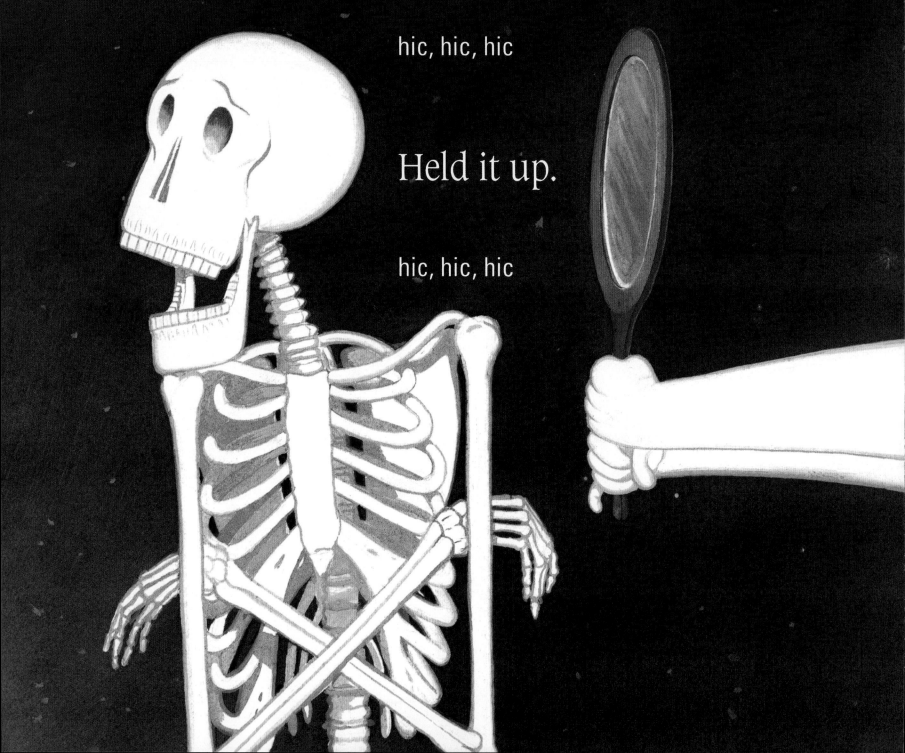

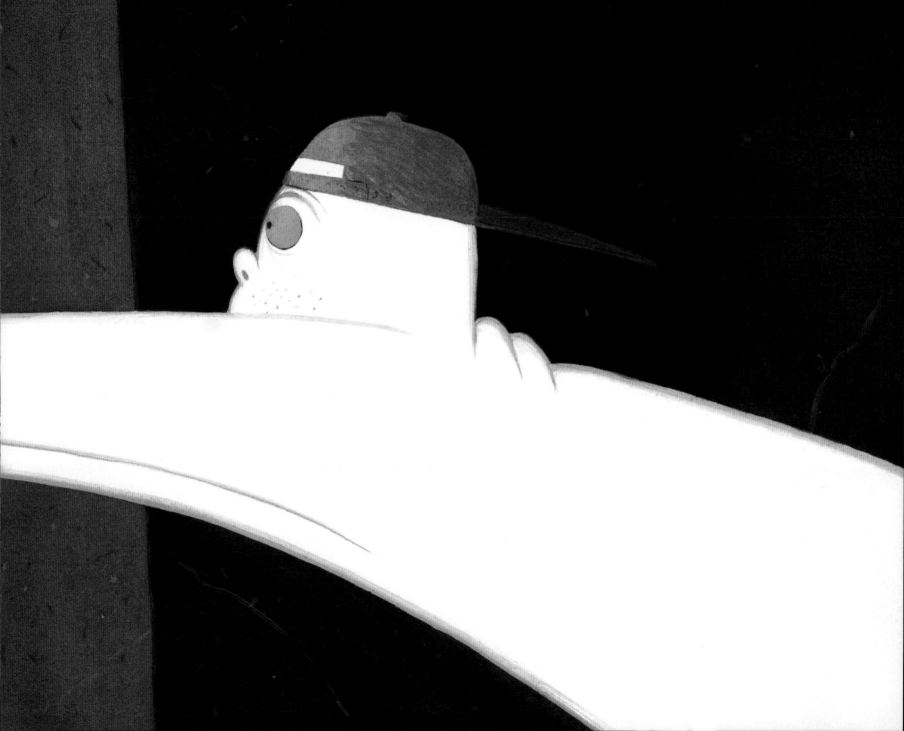

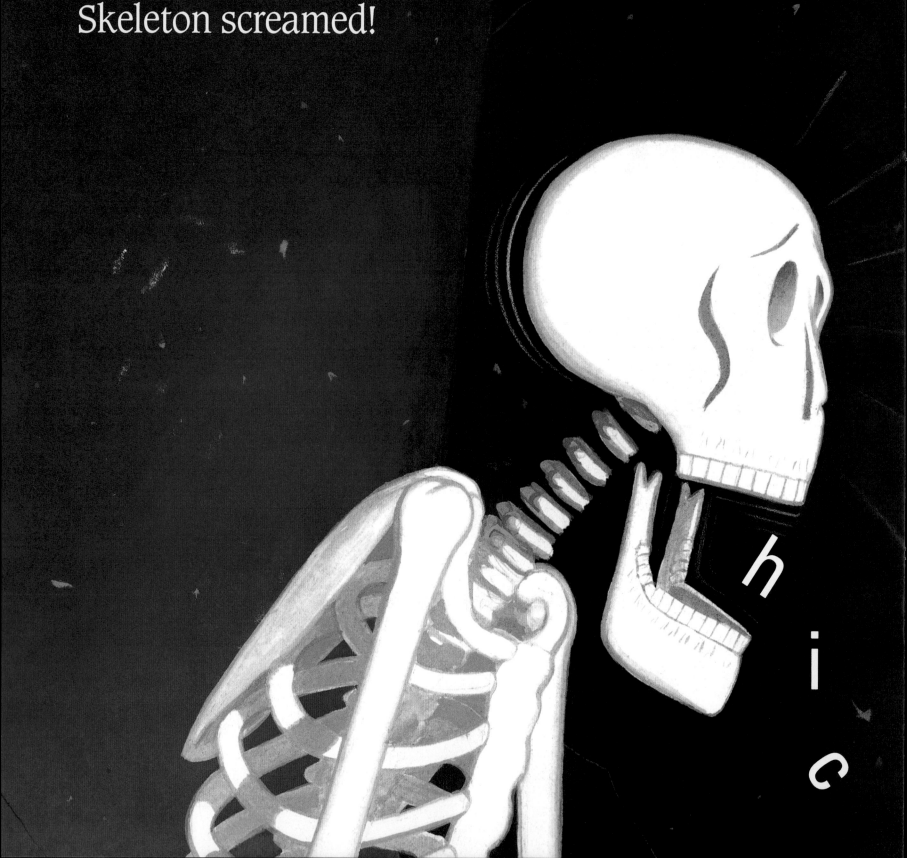

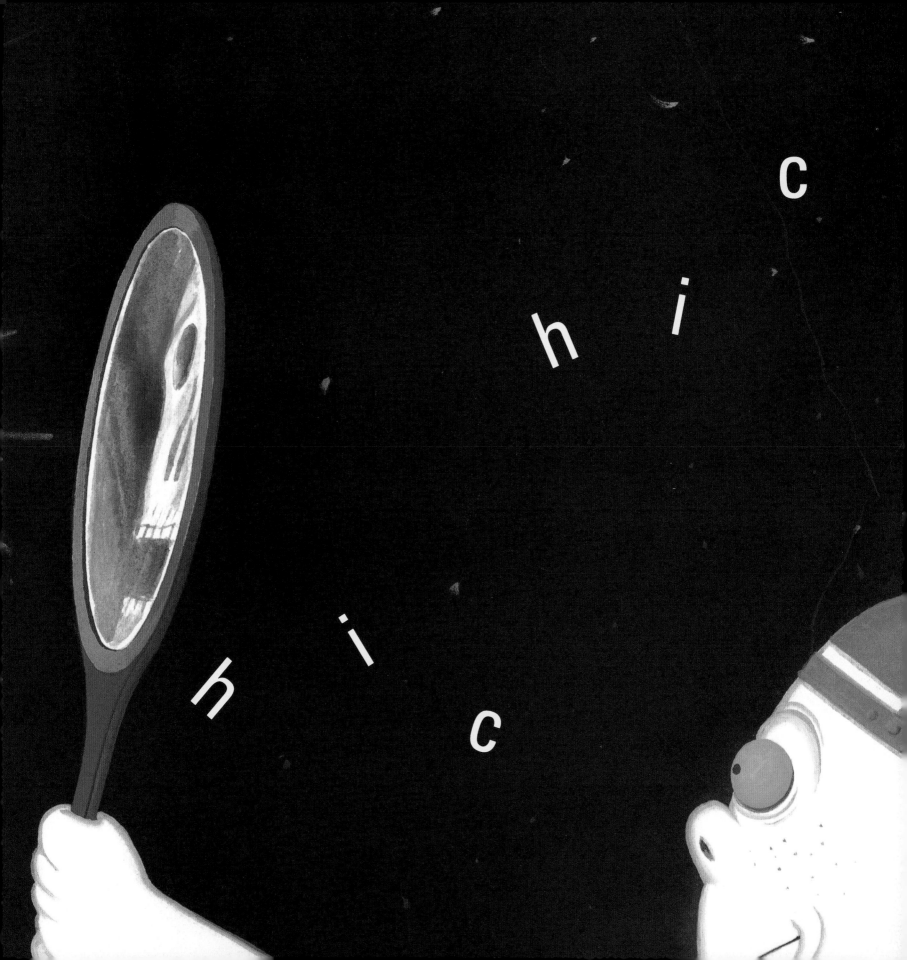

The hiccups left.

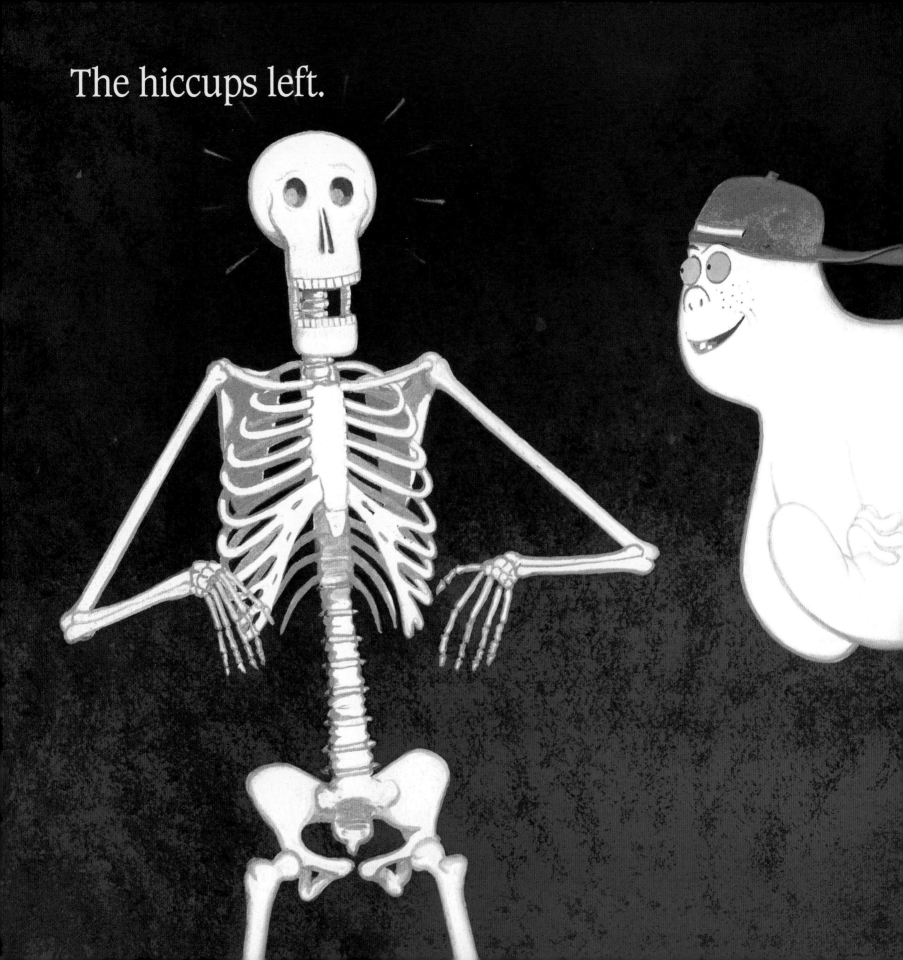

hic, hic, hic

They jumped away.

hic,

hic,

hic

Hooray!

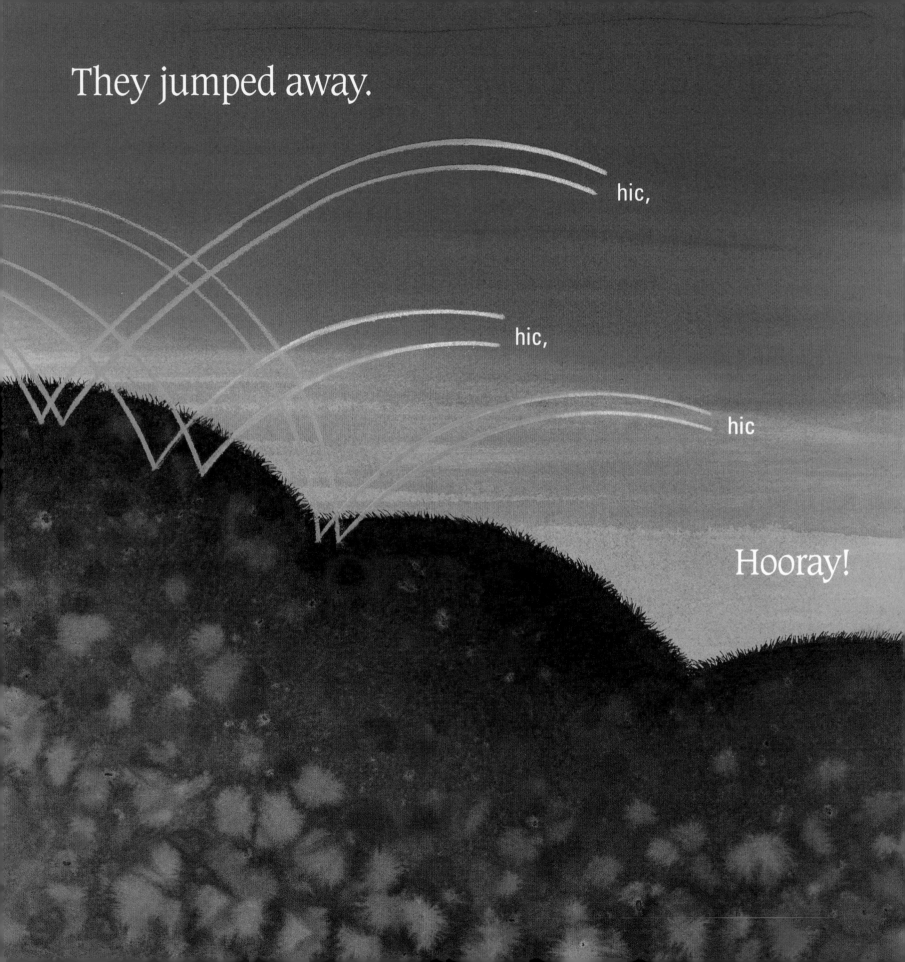